Once there was a house by the edge of a woods. The woods were deep and large and dark, filled with untrimmed plants and untamed animals, all moving freely. The house was snug and small and bright, with straight, square walls and hard, tight locks. Inside the house was a grandfather clock that called the tune, a grandfather who obeyed the clock, and a grandson named Will who obeyed his grandfather. There seemed to be as many rules in the house as there were animals in the woods. And the firmest rule was: *Don't go into the woods. The woods are strange, and people get lost in strange places.*

Then Tom Kitten came to live with them.

Now a cat is a cat, and even in a house like Grandfather's it will find a chance to obey its own rules. Tom wanted to see the woods for himself. And when the chance came, he taught his friends a new way of looking at things.

This lively and amusing tale will delight any child who loves a good story, and the imaginative pictures add a special charm of their own.

THE MYSTERY OF THE WOODS

BY MARY STOLZ

PICTURES BY URI SHULEVITZ

HARPER & ROW, PUBLISHERS
NEW YORK, EVANSTON, AND LONDON

THE MYSTERY OF THE WOODS

 For information address Harper & Row, Publishers, Incorporated, 49 East 33rd Street, New York 16, N. Y.

Library of Congress catalog card number: 64-12810

To Eric Schaefer
my friend and relation
to say nothing of my collaborator

Old Mr. Fanshaw and his grandson Will lived in a house at the edge of a woods. The woods grew so close to the house that at times it seemed it might almost come in. It would send a few little maple saplings closer, then closer, still closer, before Grandfather Fanshaw saw them and sprang with his machete to cut them back. Then a vine would come creeping over the lawn, up a wall, toward a window. Grandfather Fanshaw always spied that too, in time, and cut it back.

So the woods didn't come into the house, and Grandfather and Will didn't go into the woods.

"There are too many dark places in there and too many big trees," said Grandfather. "There are strange low plants and odd noises and wild animals, and people get lost when they wander in there. As a rule."

Grandfather Fanshaw was a cheerful, fair, friendly man, and Will was very happy with him. He listened when Will wanted to be listened to. He read aloud when Will wanted to be read to. He never said, "Later on," or, "What a silly question," or, "Will, do be quiet for a while." He knew a lot. He knew which stars were which, why the telephone works, what sort of fish swim in the Indian Ocean. He knew how to cure a fever, how to build a kite, how to make a chocolate cake.

Oh, Will loved his grandfather and was happy with him, but sometimes he wished that there were not so many rules.

Once Grandfather Fanshaw did a thing that worked out properly, he made it a rule, and once he made something a rule, he and Will never stopped doing it.

The first morning that Will had come to live with him, Grandfather had made oatmeal for breakfast. It was good, and they both said so.

"This is good," Will had said.

"So it is," Grandfather had replied happily. "Very good."

After that they had oatmeal every morning of the year for breakfast. Sometimes Grandfather put brown sugar on top. Sometimes he put honey or berries or bananas on it. But whatever was on top, it was always oatmeal underneath, and Will thought it would be nice to have something else for a change.

"Some people have bacon and eggs for breakfast," he said to his Grandfather one morning, and pushed his oatmeal bowl away.

"We have oatmeal," said Mr. Fanshaw, and pushed it back.

That was how it was.

Grandfather's neck tended to get cold. He had found long ago that a muffler was good protection against this trouble. Therefore, whenever he and Will went out, summer or winter, rain or shine, they put on their mufflers.

"My neck," said Will one day, "isn't cold. In fact, it's sort of hot."

"You can't tell when a cold snap will come," Grandfather pointed out. "I make it a rule to be prepared."

"But it's the middle of July."

"Can't be too careful," said Grandfather.

That was how it was.

There were a lot of other rules. They went to market on Tuesday and Friday, cleaned the house on Wednesday, visited the neighbors on Thursday and Saturday, went to church on Sunday, and did nothing (in accordance with the rules) on Monday.

"Why don't we clean the house on Monday and go visiting on Wednesday and do nothing on Thursday this week?" Will said once.

Grandfather moved his eyebrows together and said nothing.

There were more rules still. When they went to the library, they entered by the door on the west side and left by the door on the south. When they went out to get in the car, Will had to get in first, even if Grandfather got there first. Every night they put a stone on the garbage pail to keep the raccoons from getting in. (The raccoons got in anyway—but they had different rules.)

Still, of all the rules the one that bothered Will the most was that which said they had to do what the clock told them to.

All day long the clock directed activities in the house. The clock was a grandfather too, so Will figured he had two grandfathers, both of them telling him what to do. The clock told them when to get up, when to go to bed, when to eat, what time to go to church or downtown or on a visit.

"Some people don't do everything the clock tells them to," Will observed.

"We do," said Grandfather.

That was how it was.

Often on a bright afternoon Will would sit at the window, staring at the woods. It looked cheery just at the edge where the trees were small and slim and sunlight fell through the leaves in a flaky pattern. Now and then he saw a chipmunk dart out on the lawn and back again. He wondered if

Grandfather thought the chipmunk was a wild animal, but he didn't like to ask.

"Some people," he said, "if they lived by a woods, would take a little walk in it, in the broad daylight and not far enough to get lost or meet a wild animal."

"We won't," said Grandfather. "It's against the rules."

That was how it was. Will didn't have any rules of his own, as he figured Grandfather had enough for both of them.

One winter evening Will and Grandfather Fanshaw were sitting by the fire, toasting marshmallows. Outdoors the snow was falling. It had fallen all day, filling the woods, covering the lawns. Now it was beginning to pile softly up the windowpanes. The fire had burned quite low, and it hissed from time to time as snow found its way down the chimney. Will sighed happily as he bit on a hot, sweet, crusty marshmallow.

"Mee—wow. . . ."

"What did you say, Will?" asked Grandfather,

starting suddenly. He had been nodding toward sleep, waiting for the clock to let him go to bed. "What say?"

"I didn't say anything, Grandfather."

"Humph," said the old man. "I thought you said something like me-wow."

"Meee—wow."

"There," said Grandfather triumphantly. "Hear that?"

"I hear it," Will admitted. "Only I didn't say it." He got up and walked to the door, putting his ear against it. "I can hear the snow."

"In all my years," said Grandfather Fanshaw, "I have never heard of snow meowing."

"Then," said Will, "we'd better open the door, don't you think?"

"Now? At this time of night?" Grandfather glanced at the clock for help. "We've never done that before." The clock, which expressed itself on the hour and the half hour, stood silent and reserved because it was only twenty minutes to eight.

"Grandfather," said Will suddenly. "Why can't we do something different?"

"Different from what?"

"From what we've always done before."

"Oh, now... I don't know about that," Grandfather said. "Now, now . . . Different, did you say? But that means change. Yes, indeed. To do something different from what you've always done means you must *change*." He frowned heavily.

"Mee-wow, me-wow, *me-wow*!!!"

"Dear me," said Grandfather Fanshaw. "This is terrible. That must be a cat out there in the storm."

"Yes," said Will. "I think it must be. Because of saying meow and all."

"This one says me-wow," Grandfather pointed out. "The result of cold, perhaps. Gracious, *what* a fix we are in. We can't leave a cat out in the storm. But how can we open the door at this hour?"

"I don't see what's so wrong about changing," Will began, but his grandfather looked so anxious that he said instead, "I mean, don't you think we could make an exception and open the door and then go back to not opening it?"

"By that time the cat would be in," said Grandfather.

"Yes," said Will.

They looked at each other happily and Grandfather said, "Very well, that is what we'll do," and even as he spoke, flung wide the door.

"Hurry, hurry," he said into the night, not being able to discern quite where the meower was.

Snow swirled into the room on a cold current of air. The fire fluttered and leaped. A magazine tossed its pages. A feather Will had pulled out of the ottoman spun on its tip and danced across the rug.

"Oh, my goodness," Grandfather said, almost going out on the porch in his excitement, "why don't you come in, wherever you are? You're upsetting the entire household."

"Grandfather," said Will. "He's already in. Look."

Old Mr. Fanshaw looked.

There beside the hearth was a skinny young cat with big ears and eyes, a long thin tail, and long thin legs. It was licking snow from its back and didn't look at either Will or Grandfather until it had finished.

Grandfather hastily shut the door. "Tch, tch, tch," he tched. "All this upset. Now what are we going to do? We can't have a cat living here. It's not in the rules."

Will said nothing. He just looked at the little

cat calmly washing its face and smoothing its spiky whiskers.

The grandfather clock whirred for attention and then told everyone that now it was eight o'clock and they must all go to bed.

Grandfather Fanshaw looked at the snow piling gently against the window. He listened to the wind whistle and sigh in the chimney.

"Well," he said to Will, "we've made one exception tonight by opening the door, but we don't want to do it twice. So we will let the little cat spend one night here. In the morning he will go on his way and we will go back to ours, and everything will be the same as it always was. Change is a *very* bad thing," he repeated, giving the cat a saucer of milk. "And now it's past bedtime," he added, glancing nervously at the clock. But the clock had had its say for half an hour and now just ticked to itself.

So they went up to bed. Grandfather Fanshaw, who'd been sleepy earlier but was now wide awake, took a book with him. Although the clock could tell him when to go to bed, it had never told him when he had to sleep. Sometimes he read almost all night.

Will took a book too—one he could almost read. On second thought he took the kitten along. It had, after all, been out in the cold and snowy night and might very well like to sleep on a blanket for its one night indoors. The kitten was delighted with the arrangement. It purred for a long time, licked Will on the arm for a short time, and then spent the night *under* the blankets.

In the morning Grandfather put honey and cream on Will's oatmeal, brown sugar and butter on his own, and cream in the kitten's bowl of oatmeal.

"I wonder if cats eat oatmeal for breakfast," said Will.

"Of course they do," said Grandfather with surprise. "What else would one have for breakfast?"

"Some people have waffles and sausage," said Will.

"We have oatmeal," said Grandfather Fanshaw. "And that," he added, "is that."

The kitten seemed to agree. In any case it ate up every bit of its cereal and then meowed about for more, which Grandfather was glad to provide.

"See," said the grandfather to the grandson, "there is a cat who knows what is what."

The kitten washed its face, its tail, and one paw. Then it climbed up on the ottoman and went to sleep.

Outside, the snow had ceased falling. Smoothly it lay over lawns and bushes, sparkling in the morning sun. It had filled the woods until only the black undersides of the branches showed.

Grandfather Fanshaw walked to the window and looked out. "How beautiful it is," he said to the boy and the kitten. After a pause he added, "Also, how deep."

He and Will looked from the small sleeping kitten to the deep-drifted snow.

"Come to think of it now," said Grandfather, continuing last night's discussion, "and on the other hand, there is nothing in the rules that says we can*not* have a cat, is there?"

"Not that I know of," said Will happily.

"Nor I," said Grandfather. "And if there were such a rule, one of us would surely know about it. Well, then. And besides, this cat already knows about oatmeal. We will teach him the rest of the rules, and everything will be the same as it always was."

They named him Tom Kitten, after a cat in a book, and instructed him as to his rules, which were a little different from Grandfather's and

Will's, but not very. Tom Kitten did not, of course, have to wear a muffler. In fact, he was not to go out of the house at all.

"Not ever?" said Will.

"Not *ever,*" said Grandfather. "He'd be sure to get lost among the trees. He is a little, little cat who does not understand the mystery of the woods."

"But he'll grow up to be a big cat."

"Then he'll be a big cat who does not understand the mystery of the woods."

Tom Kitten could not go out of the house. He had to do what the clock told him to. He had to have oatmeal every morning for breakfast. And no matter how many times he said Me-wow at the front door, at the back door, at each window in turn, he could never, never get outside.

In the beginning he didn't seem to mind. He walked about the house with his head in the air and his tail in the air, leaping at shadows, at feathers, at Grandfather, and at Will. He chased his tail, hid under chairs, stalked wild enemies that

only he could see. He slept in Will's bed, napped on Grandfather's lap, and grew so big and so fast that Grandfather suggested they'd better start calling him Tom Cat pretty soon.

"All right," said Will, and he called out, "Tom Cat . . . here, Tom Cat . . . come and get your dinner, Tom Cat!"

Tom Kitten, who was sitting just outside in the hall, paid no attention.

What old Mr. Fanshaw and his grandson did not yet understand was that a cat has rules of his own, which seldom take into account the rules of people—even very nice people who provide food and warmth and laps for sleeping.

Some of Tom Kitten's rules were:

Answer to one name only.

Wash after eating.

Sleep after washing.

Eat oatmeal only if starving.

Get into any place they're trying to keep you out of.

Get out of any place that they're trying to keep you in.

Since he had been living with the Fanshaws, Tom Kitten had observed all but his last rule. He had not eaten breakfast in some time, as he was

no longer starving. He waited for dinner, and meat. He had been in every drawer, closet, and nook in the house, had explored every room and the attic and the cellar.

While Grandfather and Will watched uneasily Tom Kitten—now a young tomcat—yowled and prowled after the sun went down.

"Do you think he wants to run away from us?" Will asked.

"No," said Grandfather after a wise pause. "No, I believe he just wants to come and to go in his own fashion."

Tom Kitten stopped at the doors, at the windows, testing them with his paw to see if by chance some little oversight might afford him liberty. He had come here in the winter, and now out-of-doors grass grew green and thick, trees swayed in the west wind, and in all the world everything seemed to Tom Kitten—now crouched on the window sill, trapped behind the screen—to be free and wild except himself.

"He's awfully changed," Will said to his grandfather. "He doesn't chase his tail anymore or jump at shadows. He doesn't purr much either."

"He's angry because he can't go out," Grandfather Fanshaw said, sounding glum. "But we can't let him out because he would be sure to go into the woods, and if he goes into the woods, he'll get lost. He was just a tiny kitten when he came, and he's lived indoors ever since. He wouldn't know what to do in the woods. It's too big and mysterious for small cats and people."

Will looked out the window at the trees, which were getting dark as the sun went down. They did look strange and dangerous now, and he was glad he and Tom Kitten were safe in the house with Grandfather and the lamplight and the clock. But Tom Kitten looked over his shoulder with large, mournful eyes and turned back to stare at the night outside.

Then a most unusual thing happened. The doorbell rang.

"Gracious," said Grandfather, looking at the clock. "Who can that be?"

The clock ticked as if it knew more than it was telling, and the doorbell rang again.

Grandfather said, "Don't answer it."

"All right," said Will.

The doorbell rang again. Grandfather jumped up and stamped to the window. He peered outside, turned to Will, and said, "It's a policeman. He's ringing our doorbell. That's who it is."

"Well," said Will, "if it's a policeman, we have to open the door." He was delighted with this unexpected occurrence.

"I suppose so," said Grandfather Fanshaw grumpily, and he opened the door a crack. "What do you want, officer?" he said, and then, to be polite, "That is, good evening, officer, what may we do for you?"

"Good evening," said the policeman. "Have you seen the burglar?"

"The burglar!" Grandfather yelled. "Where's the burglar?"

"That's what I want to know," said the policeman. "Then you haven't seen him?"

"My goodness, *no,*" said Mr. Fanshaw. Will took his grandfather's hand and held it tightly, in case Grandfather should be frightened.

"I think," said the policeman, "that it would be a good idea for us to look around your house, just to be sure."

"Of course, of course," said Grandfather, opening the door wide. "Come right in, officer. Look everywhere, please. Do you think he might be hiding in the woods?" he asked, following the policeman from room to room. "There would be a lot of places for a burglar to hide in there."

"No," said the policeman, getting down on his knees to look in the cabinet under the kitchen sink. "The woods is the one place this burglar would never go. City Dan, he's called, and he hates the country. He'd be scared of the woods."

"Tch," said Grandfather. Since he was afraid of the woods himself, he didn't see how he could scoff at the burglar. Instead he said gruffly, "What's he doing out here, then? Why didn't he *stay* in the city?"

"Well," said the policeman, "that's a question. We think he was escaping from one town to another and it's quite accidental that he's in these parts at all. His car broke down."

"What a pity," said Grandfather.

The policeman wasn't sure what he meant by that and didn't like to ask. All the time they were talking, Will, Grandfather, and the policeman were covering the house, peering in closets, under beds, even out on the roof. City Dan was not to be found.

"That's that, for here," said the policeman, going back downstairs and stopping for a moment at the door. "Be sure to lock up of course."

"Of *course*," said Grandfather Fanshaw in surprise. "That's an evening rule." Just then the grandfather clock whirred and struck the hour. "In fact, now is our locking-up time to the minute."

The policeman said, "Fine, fine," and then went to his car and drove away.

"Well!" Grandfather let out a big sigh. "That was a lot of excitement. And it's made us a couple

of minutes late too. Help me to lock up, Will. You get the kitchen door while I attend to these windows."

When all was secured against the night, Will looked for Tom Kitten, to take him to bed. The cat wasn't on the windowsill or in the living room at all. Suddenly Will had a terrible thought.

"Grandfather!" he cried. "When the policeman came... we were so excited we left the front door

open! Grandfather, all that time we were looking through the house, the front door was wide open!"

Grandfather let out a groan. "Oh, my goodness. Oh, how could we have been so careless? Oh, tch, tch, tch. . . ."

"Maybe," said Will hopefully, "he didn't go out, after all? He knows the rules, Grandfather. He really does."

"He knows our rules," Grandfather said, shaking his head. "But I fear he has some of his own that conflict with ours."

"Conflict?" said Will.

"That means that when we have one rule he probably has one just the opposite. Well, just to be sure, let us look all through the house."

They looked everywhere. They looked in more places than they had looked in for City Dan—who, after all, was just a burglar they had never met, while Tom Kitten was their pet and friend and companion. But even as they were looking they knew that Tom Kitten had gone out that open door almost as soon as they'd turned their backs.

"He'll have gone into the woods," said Grandfather tensely. "Of that we can be quite, quite sure."

Will began to sniffle. "Will he get lost, Grandfather? Will we ever see him again?"

Grandfather Fanshaw cleared his throat, took a deep breath, and said, "We must go after him."

Will opened his eyes wide. "Into the woods?" he said. "Now? In the dark? At night?"

"We must go after him," Grandfather said again. "No matter what the risk. He is a cat of no experience, and it is through our carelessness that he is lost. It is our duty to find him and guide him home. Let us put on our mufflers."

And so, though it was a warm spring night, they got out their mufflers. Grandfather took his walking stick and a flashlight. Will took some dog biscuits. Tom Kitten was fond of dog biscuits, and Will thought he might need sustaining if they found him, lost and frightened in the mysterious woods.

Into the thicket they plunged, Grandfather first,

Will exceedingly close behind. The flashlight was not very strong. Its beam seemed to make shadows longer, trees taller, dark places darker. There were strange sounds on all sides of them.

"Hoot, hoot," came a voice from the treetops.

And, "Whaaah, wahooh," came a cry from a copse ahead.

"Hmm," said Grandfather. "Hmm."

Will gulped and stumbled.

On they went.

"Tom Kitten... oh, Tom Kitten!" they called. *"Where are you, Tom Kitten?"*

On and on, deeper and deeper into the dark woods. The tangle of brambles and vines grew thicker, and their feet seemed to sink in moss and ground pine. The night wind roared in the treetops, and suddenly a great crack of thunder rumbled through the sky. After it came a bolt of lightning that filled the air with light. When the lightning passed, Will and his grandfather were left in deeper darkness than they had ever before known.

Patter . . . patter . . . patter.

They listened, wondering.

Patter, patter . . . patter . . . pat-pat-patter. . . .

It was rain, hitting the high and leafy branches above them, coming down to the forest floor.

"Oh, my," said Grandfather Fanshaw. "My, my. Maybe we had better go home and look for Tom Kitten in the morning."

Will said nothing. He did not want to stay out in the wet, wild woods. But he didn't want Tom Kitten to stay out in them either. He didn't know what to say, so he said nothing.

"All right, then," said Grandfather reluctantly. "That is how we will proceed. We'll go back and return to our search in the morning."

He started off in one direction as Will started off in another.

"Wait a moment," said Grandfather. "This is the way, Will."

"I don't think so," Will said. "I think we came from this direction."

"Now, now," said Mr. Fanshaw. "We mustn't

get nervous. Or separated. Let us just stand here together and think for a minute."

They stood together in the wild, dark woods

that was getting wetter and wetter, and they thought. The more they thought, the more they knew that they didn't know where in the woods they were. They didn't know what direction they had come from or what direction they ought to go in. They didn't know where home was and there was no rule covering any of this.

We're lost, thought Will, but he didn't say it out loud, since saying a thing sometimes makes it more so.

"We're lost," said Grandfather Fanshaw, who believed in facing facts. He began to poke about with his walking stick. "Here is a place for us to stay until the rain stops."

The flashlight was growing dimmer and dimmer. By its little ray they could make out the branches of a great hemlock tree. These branches were thick and they swept toward the ground like a tent. When Grandfather led the way underneath, it was like a beautiful little cave, dry and warm and spicy smelling. The flashlight glowed in the dark like a candle, the rain rattled through the woods with a sound like falling beads. Will thought how happy he would be if it were not for being lost, and for Tom Kitten too, wet and lost and frightened out there. He hoped that Tom Kitten had found a branchy cave like this one. Without noticing what he was doing, he began to nibble on a dog biscuit. It was quite good, so he offered one to Grandfather, and they sat eating their dog biscuits in this cozy place by the faint, faint gleam of the flashlight.

The flashlight and the biscuits gave out at the same time. Then Grandfather and Will just sat.

After a long time the rain stopped and the moon came out. Its light came down through leaves and branches, making everything shine softly. Raindrops glittered on twigs and tree trunks, and as Will and Grandfather looked out from beneath the hemlock tree, a fawn came stepping along on shiny little hoofs. It disappeared as softly as if blown by a breeze. In a little while a skunk, black and white in the moonlight, ambled past. After him came a raccoon, who scrabbled for mushrooms

as he made his way through the night.

"I judge," said Grandfather, "that we are near a deer path. The animals use it at night for their comings and goings."

"They don't seem so very wild," Will said softly. "They don't seem really wild at all."

"What you mean," said Grandfather Fanshaw, "is that they don't seem fierce. An animal that doesn't live in a house or a barn is wild, even if it isn't fierce."

"But if they aren't fierce," Will asked, "why can't we come into the woods sometimes?"

"The rule is that we can't," Grandfather said in a downright voice, and they fell silent. A long time went by and then Grandfather said in a different voice altogether, "Do you suppose the rule could be wrong?" He seemed to listen to himself with surprise.

"Wrong?" said Will. *"Wrong,* Grandfather? A rule?"

"Who's to say a rule can't be wrong?" asked Grandfather Fanshaw gruffly.

Will was too accustomed to the rules to accept this astonishing statement all at once. "The rule said we'd get lost in the woods," he pointed out. "And we are lost."

"You're right, you're right, you are perfectly right," said Grandfather, so relieved for a moment to find one of the rules working out that he quite forgot to remember what a fix it had got them into.

"On the other hand," he went on after a pause, "on the other hand, Will, it seems to me that if we learned to know the woods, we wouldn't *get* lost in it. And therefore that rule would be wrong after all." He sounded rather downcast, being a man who liked rules and therefore naturally liked them to be right and to work out.

"Maybe," said Will, "some of them are right and some of them aren't?"

Grandfather considered this. "Maybe—" he

began, but at that moment they heard a soft rustle on the path and looked to see yet another animal coming toward them.

"Tom Kitten!" Will cried out in a shout of pleasure. "There's Tom Kitten!"

So it was.

Walking along with his head in the air and his tail in the air came Tom Kitten. He stopped when he heard Will and turned off the path to look under the low-sweeping branches of the hemlock tree.

"Me-wow," said Tom Kitten in greeting. *"Me-wow!"*

He swished his tail and started off, then stopped and turned to see if they were following. He was a cat who was free to stay out but now wished to go home and have something to eat, followed by a wash and a long sleep.

"I think we'd better go after him" said Grandfather Fanshaw.

"But he's lost too," said Will.

"I think not," Grandfather said firmly. "I think not."

So out they came from their branchy tent and followed Tom Kitten's white tail through the woods to home.

They found the policeman waiting for them. "I have come to reassure you," he said.

"We are quite all right," said Mr. Fanshaw. "That is, we were lost, but Tom Kitten found us."

"I see," said the policeman, who didn't because he'd never seen Tom Kitten until this minute. But he was in a hurry and did not have time to have anything explained to him. "What I came to say is, City Dan was captured five towns away from here. So we can all feel safe again."

"Well, thank you for telling us," said Mr. Fanshaw. "And now, will you take some refreshment?"

But the policeman had to hasten on to reassure more people. He said he would be happy to join them some other time, and off he went.

When Grandfather and Will and Tom Kitten were inside, they locked up as usual. City Dan might be five towns away by now, but as Grandfather said, there was no point in taking chances.

"Just because one rule is wrong," he said, "that doesn't mean they all are. Some rules are sensible and reliable. Only maybe not all of them." He was able to add this almost cheerfully because he was getting used to the idea. "In fact," he went on to his grandson, "as I was going to say when Tom Kitten came along to guide us home, maybe it's a good idea for us to go by some rules and see that some rules go by us."

They went to bed late and didn't get up till past ten o'clock the next morning. Grandfather and Will had bacon and eggs for breakfast, Tom Kitten a dish of fish, and after breakfast all three took a little stroll in the woods. Every day after that they took a walk, and each time they went in farther, because Tom Kitten always knew the way home. After a while so did Grandfather and Will.

Each evening they put a few scraps at the edge of the woods for the skunk and the raccoon, and every morning the scraps were gone. When winter came, they put out seeds for the birds and grain for the deer when the snow was heavy.

So, in a way, and after all, the woods did come to the house, just as Grandfather and Will had at last gone to the woods. It was not so mysterious after that, which is how mysteries work out . . . *as a rule.*

THE END